This igloo book belongs to:

....

D1357644

igloobooks

Published in 2017
by Igloo Books Ltd
Cottage Farm
Sywell
NN6 0BJ
www.igloobooks.com

Copyright © 2015 Igloo Books Ltd

REX001 0717
2 4 6 8 10 9 7 5 3
ISBN: 978-1-78440-979-1

Written by Melanie Joyce
Illustrated by Louise Anglicas

Printed and manufactured in China

Little Reindeer Saves Christmas

igloobooks

There was **trouble** at the North Pole.
It was nearly Christmas, but one of Santa's reindeer was sick.
"There, there," said Santa, stroking the reindeer's head.
"We'll need to find someone else to help pull my sleigh.
Any volunteers?"

"Not likely," whispered the younger reindeer, ducking down. "We're not ready for that!"

Unfortunately, one little reindeer forgot to duck.

"You'll do," said Santa.

"Me? Fly?" said Little Reindeer.
"I can't. I won't. It's not possible!"
"Yes it is," said the oldest reindeer.
"Go up to the top of that cliff and have a go.
If your nose lights up, you're flying!"

Little Reindeer went to the top of a **steep, icy cliff.** He took a big, deep breath and set off at a **trot**, then a **canter**, then a **gallop.** He got right to the edge of the cliff and took **one big leap!**

Things **didn't** quite go according to plan.
Little Reindeer's nose **didn't** light up and he **didn't** fly.
In fact, he fell with a terrible **thud** into a **huge** pile of snow.
"Ooch, ouch!" he cried, as he rolled over and over.
Soon, Little Reindeer had turned into one **giant** snowball.

Down, down, rolled the snowball, getting **bigger** and **bigger.**
"Run!" cried Santa's elves, who were carrying presents.
"Look out!" cried Santa.
"Giant snowball coming through!"

Thwack!

The giant snowball landed right in the middle of Santa's workshop.

"**What on earth are you doing?**" asked Santa.
"This is no time to be playing with snowballs.
There's work to be done."

"You try flinging yourself off a cliff and see how you like it,"
whispered Little Reindeer, brushing snow off his antlers.
Just then, the oldest reindeer said, "You need to
really **believe** that you can fly. Have another go,
but this time say, **'I can fly, I can fly!'** "

Little Reindeer trudged back up to the cliff.
He took a big breath and flung himself off.
"I can fly, I can fly!" he cried. Suddenly, he felt lighter.
He began to get **higher** and **higher** until his nose began
to **glow**. "I really **CAN** fly!" he cried and it was the
happiest moment he could ever remember.

"This is **brilliant!**" cried Little Reindeer,
swooping and **diving** and **looping**
the loop. He had no intention of coming back down.

Santa got his loudspeaker out and shouted,

"**Stop messing about up
there, Little Reindeer!**
Get down here at once!"

Santa put Little Reindeer at the back of the sleigh.
"I don't want you messing about," he said.
"I can keep an eye on you here."
Little Reindeer didn't mind. It was all so
terribly exciting. Once the sleigh was loaded,
he noticed that Santa was in a much better mood.
It was probably thanks to a **big**
piece of Mrs Claus' **delicious** Christmas cake.

Santa gave a **huge**, beaming smile and Little Reindeer felt
the tightening of his reins. It was time to go. With the sound of
hooves **padding** on snow and a great **jingling** of bells,
the sleigh flew, **WHOOSH**, into the night sky.

It was brilliant fun **whizzing** through the skies, but suddenly Little Reindeer's reins went a bit slack. The other reindeer were slowing down.

"What's the matter?" asked Santa, as the sleigh began to descend. **"We don't feel very well,"** said the other reindeer, just managing to land on a snowy roof.

Santa felt their foreheads. **"Oh, dear,"** he said. "It looks like you're ill, too. Better get you back to Mrs Claus. We must be quick though, Christmas Day will be here soon."

Back at the North Pole, the reindeer were wrapped up warm.
"It's a shame we couldn't deliver the last presents,"
said Little Reindeer. "Never mind, there's always
next year," and he plodded off to bed.

"Hold it right there," said Santa, smiling.
"It's not bedtime yet!
You're the only reindeer who can fly and isn't sick. I need you
to fly the sleigh, otherwise Christmas will be cancelled."
"Okay," said Little Reindeer, in a small, squeaky voice.

Little Reindeer felt **really** nervous.
"Don't worry," said Mrs Claus, giving him
a special piece of Christmas cake.
"This will do the trick. It works for Santa
every time." Suddenly, Little Reindeer
began to feel **much** better.

He was absolutely raring to go
and that is exactly what he did.
In fact, he went like a rocket.
"By golly," said Santa,
laughing, as he and
Little Reindeer flew off to
deliver the very **last** presents.

After a long night, Santa and Little Reindeer
arrived back at the North Pole.
Everyone **clapped** and **cheered**.
"Oh, it was nothing," said Little Reindeer,
blushing, but Santa disagreed.
"You are a very **brave** and **loyal** reindeer,"
he said. **"I'm very proud of you."**

Well Done, Little Reindeer!

Little Reindeer looked up at Santa with a tear in his eye.
"Thank you, Santa," he said. "That's the **best** Christmas present ever.
Merry Christmas, everyone!"

Merry Christmas

Goodbye